Cotton-Wooleena

Cotton-Wooleena

Laurence Housman

Illustrated by Robert Binks

Doubleday & Company, Inc.,
Garden City, New York

ISBN: 0-385-05673-7   Trade
0-385-06649-X   Prebound
Library of Congress Catalog Card Number 79-157429
Illustrations Copyright © 1974 by Doubleday & Company, Inc.
Text Copyright © 1967 by Jonathan Cape Limited

Cotton-Wooleena

The King. Not our King, neither the last nor the present nor the future; but just the King as he happened to be of that particular country, and time, and place, somewhere in the age in which we live now. And as he does not wish what has now become of him to be known, I call him "the King" for short.

He lived—as he lives still—in the days of trousers, and automobiles, and phonographs; and on any ordinary day, as he took his walk through the park, you would not know that he was the King unless you happened to notice how carefully all the policemen and park keepers saluted as he went by, and how at a short distance behind walked two beautifully dressed detectives invisibly armed to the teeth to protect him in case of need.

A little boy, who did not know him by sight, stopped him one morning to ask the time, and the detectives slid swiftly to the rescue; but the King waved them off.

"I don't need you," he said. "I can tell the little boy the time as correctly as you can." And pulling out his beautiful gold watch, he told the little boy that his was five and a half minutes to eleven, at which news the little boy set off running as hard as he could go. And the King stood looking after him, and smiled, and said: "I hope he gets there in time."

But the detectives were too much be-wildered and upset to say anything; for it was a most upsetting thing that in the park of his own capital the King should have been stopped and asked the time before the detectives could step in and prevent it; and if it got to the ears of the superintendent of police it would be as much as their places were worth that they should have allowed it to happen.

I have told this incident at the beginning of my story to show that the King was a much more simple and human person than his official protectors knew or even wished him to be; because if you are human you are

3

apt to break rules; and if—in a court that is made up entirely of rules and ceremonies— the King himself begins to break them, where are you—where is it going to end?

Now that is the question which this King, surrounded by rules and ceremonies from morning till night, was always asking himself: "Where am I?" and "Where am I going to end?" So often, in the midst of these things— if the truth must be known—he felt himself lost; just as, first of all, he had felt himself lost on the day of his coronation, when, having had to discard waistcoat and trousers, and tail coat, and top hat, and socks, and walking shoes, he stood and looked at himself in the long mirror of his dressing room and saw a strange figure in white satin tights, and crimson tunic, and an immense cloak, all cloth of gold mingled with ermine, and on his head the crown which had been worn by the King's ancestors for twenty generations before him. And because the crown was a little large for him, it had been stuffed with an extra lining of fur, which, to begin with, was soft and comfortable, but presently grew hot, making him think how very much he would have preferred a cabbage leaf or the cool rind of a cucumber instead. But fur being the proper lining for a crown, fur it had to be. And as he stood and looked at himself in all these things, the King felt lost. "Where am I?" he said to himself. "What has become of me?"

During the ceremony he had so many things to think about, and remember, and do that he forgot himself altogether; and it was only when all was over and he was once more alone in his dressing room that he had time to take another look at himself, when, staring at the strange figure which stood in the glass before him, he cried in wonder: "Good gracious! Where am I? What has become of me?"

He took off his crown; he laid down the scepter and the orb, putting them all on his dressing table; but while attending carefully to the crown, he was inattentive to the orb, which, because of its shape, rolled and fell on to the floor.

It fell rather heavily, and when he picked it up there was a dent in it. "Dear, dear! Look what you've done now!" he said to himself. "And how am I going to put it right?"

The dent was near the top, on which stood a gold ornament—a dove set with jewels, and in the dove's beak was a scroll bearing the words: *J'y suis, j'y reste*. Examining it carefully, he thought, "I wonder if it unscrews? If it does, I can push out the dent from the inside, so that no one will know." He felt rather like a child with a broken toy, but safer, knowing that nobody would dare to enter his presence without knocking first for permission. So, taking hold of the jeweled bird, he began twisting it, and after a time very slowly and very stiffly it began to unscrew. In about a dozen turns he had screwed it off, and there was the screw hole nearly an inch wide for him to stick his finger through. As he did so he encountered within a soft substance, which yielded as he touched it; and after a good deal of poking and pulling he got a little of it to come out. It was a tag of cotton-wool. Taking hold of it, he started to pull, and, in a long thin trail, the cotton-wool began to emerge, first inches, then almost amounting to yards. It seemed

7

that the orb of the realm had been tightly stuffed with cotton-wool.

The King was getting quite interested and wondering how much more there was to come, when a small plaintive voice from within cried: "Oh, please don't pull my tail so!"

The King, very much astonished, stopped pulling; he put his eye to the hole but could see nothing. Then, since he could not let the situation stop at that, "Who's in there?" he inquired. "Who are you?"

"If you'll let go of my tail, I'll tell you," said the voice from within. The King loosed the cotton-wool. Instantly it whipped back like a snake into its hole and disappeared. In its place, out came a head. "Why can't you let me alone?" said the head reproachfully. "I was doing nothing to you."

"This orb happens to belong to me," explained the King, "and you are inside it. Perhaps you don't know I'm the King. If I said 'Get out!' I should be within my rights."

"Oh, would you?" retorted the head. "If you ever say 'Get out!' to me, you'll have the surprise of your life! Call yourself King indeed! Much of a King you'd be then."

The King was not accustomed to being spoken to in that way, especially not on his Coronation Day. "Who are you?" he inquired.

"Cotton-Wooleena is my name," answered the head, "the Fairy Cotton-Wooleena."

"A fairy, eh?" said the King. "So such things do still exist? I should like to see more of you."

"Things indeed!" retorted the Fairy. "If you saw more of me perhaps you'd see too much of me. Be thankful for small mercies. *J'y suis, j'y reste,* as your own motto says. Here I am, and here I mean to stay, unless you insist that I am to get out. Don't say it unless you mean it, or you'll be sorry for it."

"Heaven forbid," said the King, "that I should turn a lady out from anywhere, still less a fairy! But staying in there must be very dull. What do you do? How do you manage to pass the time?"

"I rule the kingdom, of course," replied the Fairy. "And I don't pass the time; time passes me. I've been here for three hundred years without ever changing."

10

"Dear me!" said the King. "I didn't know cotton-wool had been invented so long."

"You mean 'discovered,'" replied the Fairy. "I existed long before I was discovered. So did America, so does everything. You may only discover yourself to be a fool years after you've been one."

"And I only discover you to be a very rude person," replied the King, amused to find what a crabby character he was dealing with, "after it's become so much a habit that you yourself are probably not aware of it. Wouldn't change of air do you good?"

"If I changed," said the Fairy, "you'd be nowhere. I've been keeping you and your ancestors in cotton-wool for years without you knowing it. It was my special discovery that to wrap up the insides of people and things in cotton-wool was just as effective as wrapping up outsides. But if I once came out into the open and made cotton-wool the rage, without end or limit, you'd find the difference. As it is, I just keep things as they are—or pretty nearly—so far as you are concerned. A day may come when you'll see too much of me. Now I've talked to you enough.

11

Put my top on again. Don't trouble about that dent, I'll mend it myself. And in future, don't make any mistake: you may think that it's you that is ruling the country, and keeping things in their place, but it isn't—it's me!"

So saying, she drew her head into the hole and disappeared, without any ceremony.

The King was more polite. "Good-by!" he called after her. "Some day I hope we may meet again." Then he took up the dove and screwed it on again, and as he did so he perceived that the dent was already mended; so when the Master of Ceremonies returned and knocked and was admitted, he had nothing to confess to him.

But all the same he had a surprise for him. The Master of Ceremonies had brought with him a box padded inside and lined with red velvet, in which he proceeded to pack the crown, the orb, and the scepter, to wait till the next occasion when they would be called for. Having locked the box, he was just going to walk off with it when the King said: "Thank you. I will keep that myself."

The Master of Ceremonies looked very

much astonished. "But they won't be wanted, sir," he said; "they won't be wanted again till you are—till the next coronation."

"You are mistaken," said the King; "I want them. I have a use for them."

"But, sir," objected the Master of Ceremonies, "they are very valuable; unless kept in strict custody they might be stolen."

"They can be insured," said the King. "Insure them for a million pounds, and I will pay the insurance. We have had them out today to impress the populace, and the diplomats, and the illustrated newspapers. I want to keep them to impress myself. I have an idea that if I use them in private constantly three times a day, before and after meals or when I get up and when I go to bed—I have an idea that they may help me to behave as a King ought to behave; otherwise—being new to the business—I may forget how. It need be no trouble to anyone except myself; I will keep the box under my bed, and always locked, and I will only take them out in private, so that nobody will see, and burglars will not get to know about them."

14

The Master of Ceremonies said: "But such a thing has never been done, sir!"

"No, but it is going to be," replied the King. "Take the box up to my bedroom, and give me the key. And if you'd like to let me have a chamois and an old toothbrush and some powder to keep them polished, I will see to it regularly."

Awed by such acquaintance with practical details, the Master of Ceremonies said: "Your Majesty has the most marvelous and encyclopedic knowledge of any monarch I have ever met. But it is contrary to all constitutional practice that I should do any such thing. Your Majesty must excuse me."

"Certainly," said the King. "I will do it myself." And taking the box under his arm, he walked off with it and put it under his bed himself. Then he came back and said: "Oh, please do give me the key." Which the Master of Ceremonies accordingly did.

But as he did so the King saw a look in his eye which caused him to doubt. And so, returning again to his bedroom, he unlocked the box, and taking out the crown and the orb and the scepter, he put in their place

15

a pair of dumbbells which he had left off using, a small pistol, a silver inkstand that he could easily spare, and a large crystal paperweight. These were things which in a palace replete with art treasures of very differing values would never seriously be missed, and as they were much of the same weight as the articles they replaced, the King felt fairly confident that the substitution he had effected would never be discovered. To make doubly sure, he filled up the keyhole with tooth powder and sealing wax and sealed it with his own seal. He then put crown, orb, and scepter into the drawer where he kept his collars and handkerchiefs, locked it, and felt safe.

About a month later, he was much amused to find that under his bed a facsimile box had been substituted, containing—when he opened it—a perfect imitation of the coronation regalia, so good that it would have deceived even a professional burglar, and must in the making have cost quite a considerable sum.

So the dumbbells and the inkstand and the paperweight, having the royal seal upon them, had gone down unexamined into the strong room of the palace, there to await his demise and the next coronation. And if, in the meantime, restoration did not take place, what a surprise it would be for them when that day came! It made him quite sorry that he himself would not be there to see the expression on the face of the Master of Ceremonies, or hear what sort of an excuse he would make for himself at the discovery. And then it struck him that he ought to have put in a note explaining that the thing was his own doing, so that the Master of Ceremonies should not have to suffer for his fault.

"Never mind," he said to himself. "I will leave a memorandum along with my will to explain matters." So there and then he sat down and wrote as follows:

> When you find a pair of dumbbells,
>   And a small pocket pistol,
> A solid silver inkstand,
>   And a paperweight of crystal,
> Instead of the regalia,
>   Don't think it was a theft
> Or anybody's failure

To take care of what was left.
They are just as I arranged them;
So I make this memorandum—
It was I myself who changed them.
To my heir you'll please to hand
them.

The King had never before in his life written poetry. He was quite pleased with himself; he signed with a flourish, and then, opening the desk in which he kept his private papers, he attached it to his will; and having thus quieted his conscience, he put it away and thought no more about it.

But about the real genuine regalia which he kept locked in his collar drawer he continued to think a good deal. It had just the effect upon him which he had expected it to have. It gave him something—a sort of royal standard to live up to; night and morning he would get it out and refresh himself with it; he would put on the crown and wear it while he trimmed his beard. One day he tried taking his bath with crown, orb, and scepter for accompaniment.

It made him feel kingly to the bone. After

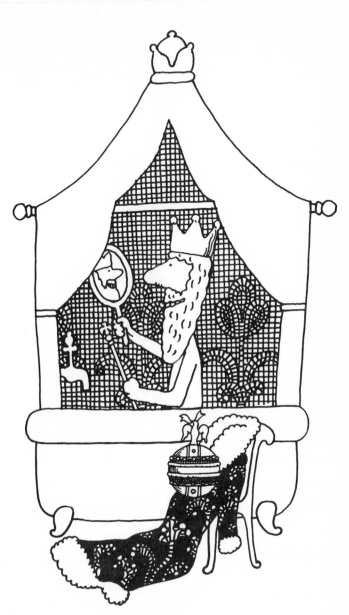

19

a while his crown became like a familiar spirit to him. He tried also going to bed with it; but though it went better with his night-shirt than any of his other clothes, on the pillow it proved uncomfortable. His orb, however, was a much more pleasant and accommodating bedfellow; sleeping with it became a habit. He liked the feeling of it, and the romance—the sense that it contained a fairy; and often as he lay holding the orb snuggled to his breast he would listen for any sound of movement inside; but the Fairy Cotton-Wooleena was true to her name: close and cozy she lay with her long tail wrapped tightly around her, not attending apparently in the least to anything that went on in the outside world.

But it happened one day that the King had been having a good deal of trouble with his ministers. A constitutional crisis had arisen over which he and they differed: for the King, as you may have noticed or surmised, was without a wife—was, in fact, a widower, his wife having died just before he came to the throne. But time having passed, and his grief abated, he had recently begun thinking of marrying again. And it was over this—his choice of a second wife—that he and his ministers had been having their difference of opinion. For the King, wishing only to marry privately, had let his choice fall on the very excellent lady who was his housekeeper. She being the one of all people who made him most comfortable in other respects, he had come to the conclusion that she would also be the most comfortable person for him to marry. And having quite made up his mind about it, he had that day taken out a special license, and in order to put an end to further discussion, had shown it to his ministers. Whereupon his ministers had got up in a body and resigned—had said, at least, that they would resign if the thing happened. To which the King had replied: "Very well, appeal to the country; have a general election on the question, or a referendum. It will be very interesting. And if I get beaten I'll abdicate."

And there—as though that settled the matter—he had left it; and while his astonished ministers retired to a sleepless night of perturbations and alarms, he had gone to his own bed and slept on it quite undisturbed.

That undisturbed sleep was the undoing of him. For had he been wakeful, he might then have seen what happened, and escaped from the entanglement while it was in process. Whereas, from sleeping too well, he only woke to the results. For in the middle of the night—his orb lying beside him between turn-down and pillow—the dove that formed the top of it began softly to unscrew, and out came—not the Fairy, but the tail. Softly, slowly, silently, her cotton-wool tail, openly elongating, began moving under the sheet toward him. Presently it touched, and sensitively feeling its way in, started to wind around him. Under, over, and around, like a cocoon it coiled him in a soft and sensible embrace; and with soft and sensible dreams having lulled his brain during the rest of that night, at dawn—retiring as silently as it had come—it returned once more to its place of concealment. Then the Fairy, putting out her hand, took hold of the top and screwed it on again from inside.

An hour later, when the King woke, he

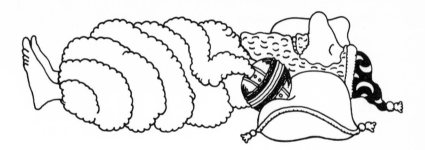

found himself cured of any wish or intention to marry his housekeeper, and the constitutional crisis was over.

So, that time at any rate, without the King knowing anything about it, the Fairy had got her way. The license disappeared, and the King made no inquiry as to what had become of it. The housekeeper also disappeared; finding herself no longer in request for seeing to the King's domestic comfort—pouring out his coffee, mending his socks, and such things—and being a self-respecting person, she had left without notice. And so well had the Fairy Cotton-Wooleena done her work, smothering up his affections in cotton-wool, that the King did not even inquire what had become of her; and, the ministers withdrawing their resignations without further remark, everything went on as before, in the proper traditional way, with the Fairy Cotton-Wooleena presiding and directing in secret as she had always done for almost three hundred years.

But though the Fairy had been against him that time, next time she was for him. For before long another constitutional crisis arose, and this time it was not the King's doing, but his ministers'.

What they were actually proposing to do hardly matters; it was one of those foolish things in which only grown-up people concern themselves—call it "a reform," if you like; the ministers considered it an improvement, the King regarded it as a breach of his prerogatives. Prerogatives, you may like to know, are things that a King has a right to do but never does do: they are always in fact done for him. And what the ministers were now proposing to do was to make this fact become law. The King wished still to have the law on his side, and that is all about it.

And so, once more, in the Council Chamber the King and his ministers differed about what should be done: immemorial tradition was being disturbed, and the King, feeling that he had a duty to all that the Crown stood for, was disturbed by it also.

That night he heard inside the orb a tiny tapping sound: the Fairy was awake. He got up and, as a mark of respect, before letting the lady out, put on slippers and dressing gown. Then he unscrewed and took off the top; a moment later out came the Fairy's head.

"Very glad to meet you again," said the King. "You come in the nick of time." He started to explain, but the Fairy stopped him. "Do you suppose," she said, "that I don't know what's been going on? Didn't I tell you it was I who ruled the kingdom, not you? Well, you want these ministers of yours brought to heel. They shall be. You take me down with you to the Council Chamber to-morrow, and when you are all seated, then (under the table so that they don't see) unscrew and let me out. That'll settle them!"

She said no more; she drew in her head; the interview was over.

With his mind much relieved, the King slept soundly, and went down to the Council

Chamber in the morning with a confidence which he generally lacked.

As soon as political grace had been said at the council board, the King—under cover of the table cloth—unscrewed the dove of peace, and Cotton-Wooleena crept out tail first and did the rest. Under the table she did it; nobody saw.

A faint odor of camphor and musk began to pervade the room, and gradually the brains of the rebellious ministry grew fusty and slow. Timidity crept into their counsels, tradition resumed its weight; the pendulum of change swung back to an even balance; prerogative prevailed, the new proposals were withdrawn. All was once more as it had always been and should always remain in a country where change had hitherto been regarded as revolution.

The King's respect for the powers of the Fairy Cotton-Wooleena was now immense. It was evident that she really did rule the kingdom; he had hardly believed it before.

That night he felt so kingly that, in spite of the accompanying discomfort, he put on his crown, got into bed, and—without intending—went to sleep in it.

27

He woke next morning to see his valet, who had come to call him, staring at him in dazed astonishment. The King realized what had happened; he rose to the occasion.

"Pray do you see anything odd about me?" he inquired.

Thus challenged, the man could only stutter and stammer: "No, no, Your Majesty!"

"That is as well," said the King. "If you had, I should have been obliged to suppose that you were drunk, and were seeing things which you would not see if you were sober."

The King was so accustomed to having his word accepted that he considered this sufficient. What the man had seen he was supposed not to have seen; and as this is a faculty in which the servants of royalty are specially trained, he had no doubt that the man, accepting the traditions of his trade, would take the hint and say no more about it.

And I dare say he didn't, and that nobody else heard of it. What happened next may have been merely a coincidence, but, anyway, it happened the next night. The King woke up and found a burglar in his room.

And having never before seen a burglar at work, he lay and watched him with half-closed eyes—still pretending to be asleep—with great interest.

He watched the man taking his watch and rings from the dressing table, next out of one of the drawers an assortment of studs and cuff links. Then, advancing with his jimmy to the wardrobe, he tried the drawer in which the King's collars and handkerchiefs were lying—the drawer which he always kept locked, because in it lay the regalia of the realm.

This wouldn't do at all. Unable any longer to remain a passive onlooker, "Ahem!" cried the King, and sat up in bed.

The burglar sprang sharply around, and with jimmy raised came running toward him. His attitude was distinctly threatening.

"Don't hurt me," said the King gently. "I'm not going to hurt you."

"If you make so much as a pig's whistle," said the man, "you are done for."

"I don't know how pigs do whistle," said the King. "And anyway, I'm far too much interested in what you are doing to have any wish to disturb you. How ever did you manage to get in?"

"That's my affair," said the man.

"Not yours alone," replied the King. "When the Chief Commissioner of Police hears of this tomorrow morning, he will either have to resign or commit suicide, unless I can give him a satisfactory explanation. Surely you don't wish that to happen?"

"I don't care what happens," replied the man, "so long as I get safe away with what I've come for."

"And what have you come for?" inquired the King.

"Anything I can get."

"Anything I can let you have, I shall be most happy," replied the King. "Now, under my bed, you will find a box containing the crown jewels, and if you will look in that drawer over there, the bottom one to the right, you will find the key."

"None of your tricks," said the man. "I'm not to be kidded like that. Soon as I go under the bed to look for it you'll be ringing the bell, I suppose? Not much!"

"I am not kidding you in the least," said

the King. "I will get under the bed for it myself. And if you'd like to hold a pistol at my head while I am doing so you are welcome."

As he spoke, the King got up and put on his dressing gown, having first taken the precaution to put the orb, which as usual he had taken to bed with him, under his pillow.

"You see," he went on, "the crown jewels are no use to me. I shall never wear them again. They are merely waiting for my successor."

The King got out the box, found the key, and gave it to the burglar.

"You can either open it yourself," he said, "or I will open it. And I can assure you that you are perfectly welcome to anything that it contains."

"You mean," cried the astonished burglar, "that you give them to me?"

"I give them to you," said the King, "for your very own. What do you mean to do with them?"

And then a happy thought occurred to him and he said: "If you will ride through the park in them tomorrow, I will give you a

31

32

check for a hundred pounds. I really mean it," said the King, seeing the man hesitate. "I am not deceiving you."

"And what will become of me?" inquired the man. "Won't they nab me for wearing 'em?"

"Of course they will," said the King. "Then I shall come as a witness for the defense, and I shall say that I gave them to you. I am really offering you a very good bargain. Do you not realize that those jewels are far too large and valuable for you ever to be able to dispose of them otherwise? If you were to try with even the smallest of them, you would get caught at once. Whereas, if I commit the indiscretion of giving them to you, I assure you that the government will be ready to grant you a large pension for life rather than let the case come into court at all."

"Well, if you aren't the queerest customer I ever came across!" said the man.

"I shouldn't wonder," replied the King. "You are not accustomed to meeting crowned heads in the privacy of their own bedrooms, when they have no special call for behaving themselves as they are expected to behave, and as they don't want to behave. You see me now as nobody has ever seen me before, indulging in a wild fit of irresponsibility. I am now trying not to let myself think what is going to happen as the result of all this. But that I will stand by you whatever happens, I give you my word. If you knew the boredom it is to live a life of rules and ceremonies, you would understand with what a delightful diversion you are providing me. I am going, for once, to make myself impossible, in order to see by what means and with what trouble and expense they will manage to make me possible again.

"And now, if you agree, let me get back to bed and resume my slumbers. I will lend you a suitcase, a latchkey, a ladder, anything you'd like to suggest that will facilitate your escape. And if it is any satisfaction to you, you may have the satisfaction of knowing that you have made my life seem to me for a little while really worth living. I am looking forward very much—a thing I seldom do—to what is going to happen tomorrow."

When the burglar had gone the King got

back into bed again; but he was so excited and interested in wondering what would happen tomorrow that he could not sleep. But he was happy, so happy that he lay as quiet as a lamb; anyone might have thought he was sleeping.

Apparently the Fairy Cotton-Wooleena thought so. Under his hand that was resting on it, the King felt the dove give a soft turn; it continued to turn; the Fairy was letting herself out. Very cautiously the King switched on the light and watched. He watched, wondering what it could mean. Presently the dove fell off and lay upon its side, and, tail first—indeed, tail only—he saw the Fairy beginning to emerge.

The tail began feeling its way toward him, creepy-crawly over the sheet like a white woolly blindworm—could such a thing ever have existed—it came searchingly along with soft undulating motion till it touched him.

Suddenly the King remembered the scene in the Council Chamber, when with circulating tail the Fairy had quelled for him a whole board of ministers. Was she now trying the same thing on him? Startled by the thought, he jumped up and sprang out of bed.

The Fairy must have heard him, and swifter than snake or eel when it darts upon its prey, the tail—like a yardstick gone mad—sprang after him. The room was a large one; the King began running around it, but wherever he went, after him exuberantly came the tail; writhing, twisting, heaving, swirling, it covered the carpet with a repeating pattern that seemed to have no end. And the pattern moved; the King caught his foot in it; at once the coil tightened. He was held, he could not escape. Desperately he snatched up his nail scissors and, stooping to his bound ankle, gave the tail a snip.

"Ow!" screamed the Fairy. The hollow orb resounded her cry. Back into its safe keeping whipped all of the tail that was left. The remainder, the cut-off portion, still lay about on the carpet, squirmless and without motion: all its vice and virtue had gone out of it.

Picking his way across it, the King returned to his bed; he expected to see the Fairy's head come out, and was prepared to exchange words with her. But the Fairy gave no sign and made no sound. No doubt she had had the shock of her life, and was thinking about it.

The King put his mouth to the screw hole. "Madam," he said firmly, "you let me alone, and I will let you alone!" And so saying he picked up the dove of peace and screwed it on again—screwed it firmly—and then stood thinking what he should do next. Was "firmly" enough? No, he must make sure, for Cotton-Wooleena, with her fairy hands, had some way of her own for screwing it off from the inside.

So he went to his bureau and got out some strong string and a large stick of sealing wax, and having tied the dove permanently into position to prevent further unscrewings, he sealed it into fixity with so many seals that when all was done it presented to the eye nothing but a network of knotted strings filled up with sealing wax. Then he put it back into his collar drawer, along with the other regalia, locked it up, and so to bed again, this time to sleep.

He woke up to find his manservant walking

about the room entangled in cotton-wool. The man was doing his best to pretend not to notice it, lest his sobriety should be called in question. But this time the King felt that a certain amount of explanation was necessary, so he said:

"You had better gather that up. It came out of something."

The man did as he was told, and going down to the servants' quarters carrying a bundle on his shoulder bigger than himself, he reported that the King had been playing in the night with a stuffed elephant which had come undone. On the truth of that statement being questioned by certain members of the staff, all he said was, "Well, how else can you account for all this?" And nobody could; his explanation stood the test of being less improbable than all the others which were put forward as alternatives. It gave the palace servants a great deal to talk about; for now the man admitted what he had seen previously, and putting this and that together they began to have a feeling and a fear that the King was not quite right in his head. In another twenty-four hours that fear had extended to the whole nation.

This was the day when the King—doubtfully, but still with expectation and hope—picked up his morning newspaper to read, in headlines extending across six columns:

AMAZING THEFT OF
CROWN JEWELS.
THIEF CAUGHT
WEARING THE CROWN.
UNEXPLAINED MYSTERY.

The King read with delight. Yes, the thief had kept his word; first had ridden into the park carrying a bag; and then, without any concealment, before the eyes of all, had opened the bag and taken out crown and

39

scepter, and, putting the one upon his head, had used the other to goad his nag—first into a smart canter, then into a wild gallop with the whole body of the park police force tearing after him.

Of course they caught him. The scene was graphically described; but the mystery remained! The man's explanation was not given in this or any other paper. About the King's check and the King's promise not a word. And the accused was due to appear in the police court that day. Very interesting.

The King wondered if he himself would be able to get there. All possible obstacles would, he felt sure, be put in his way; but, of course, he was going to keep his word; of that there would be no question.

But there was question. It came when the first obstacle presented itself. The Master of Ceremonies, white and palpitating, came to break the awful news—news which had reached him a good many hours earlier, and had led to certain investigations which had now to be admitted.

The Master of Ceremonies began by stating the case, much as the papers had stated it, but with interrogation in his tone.

The King did his best to satisfy him. "Yes, yes, yes," he said, "it's all right. I gave them to him. He came to see me the night before last—'broke in,' I think, are the right words for it—and took them in the box which, as I told him, was under my bed. You remember warning me that such a thing might happen. Well, it has. To save him from committing a crime I gave them to him—before he asked for them. The only right and Christian thing to do, eh?"

The Master of Ceremonies seemed hardly to have heard him. "But where, where, Your Majesty, are the crown jewels—the real crown jewels? What has become of them? Those in the box were only imitation."

"Are you quite sure?" said the King.

"Oh, quite! Your Majesty, we had to do it. Your Majesty must pardon me! When Your Majesty insisted upon keeping them, we effected a substitution. But now—on hearing the news—wishing to verify—it was necessary for the prosecution to know, and to appease the public mind—so, wishing to verify, I went and myself opened—with some difficulty—since Your Majesty had put sealing wax into the lock—I opened the other box where the real crown jewels should have been. And there I found—oh, Your Majesty!—nothing of the kind: only a paperweight, and a pistol, and a pair of dumbbells, and an inkstand. It is terrible, terrible! I cannot conceive how such a thing can have happened. It must have been done on the very day—before, before any substitution could be effected."

"My dear man," said the King, "don't distress yourself any longer. This is how it happened." He got up, went to his bureau, took out his will, and, detaching the appended document, gave it to the Master of Ceremonies to read.

And the court official, with eyes popping out of his head in consternation and astonishment, read the verses which the King had written.

"Rather good, don't you think?" inquired the King, when he saw that the other had done reading. "I never knew before that I could write poetry. I suppose the situation inspired me."

Whatever the situation may have done for the King in the past, it did not inspire the Master of Ceremonies now.

"But, Your Majesty," he exclaimed, "this is too awful! If Your Majesty effected the substitution, where are the crown jewels now?"

"Ah!" said the King. "Let's go down to the court and see."

"The court?"

"The police court, I mean. I promised I would be a witness."

The hair of the Master of Ceremonies so stood up on end as he heard this that it almost came off.

"But, Your Majesty," he cried, "that is impossible!"

"I thought you would say so," replied the King, "but I assure you it can be done, and I am going to do it."

The Master of Ceremonies, a trained adept in the reading of the royal eye, looked and saw that the King meant it. With a respectfully stifled cry he turned and fled from the apartment.

The King heard him descending the stairs

43

in great haste, beating his breast as he ran. Evidently he had gone with a purpose.

"I must lose no time," thought the King.

He put on his coat and hat, and descended to the palace entrance. He passed nobody on the way—not an attendant was in sight. This was very strange. He came to the door and found it locked. He rang a bell to summon an attendant. Nobody answered.

He turned aside, passed through corridors, came to another door: that also was locked. Three more doors he tried in turn; they were all locked. Nowhere could he see an attendant. Six or eight bells had he rung, and no one had answered. He was a prisoner in his own palace.

"This won't do," he said to himself, "this won't do at all! I must teach them a lesson."

He returned to his room, locked the door, put on his oldest suit of clothes—a suit which he wore when he wished to go about the streets of the city incognito, and then swiftly and deliberately cut off his beard and his mustache, and five minutes later presented so smooth-shaven an appearance that when he looked in the glass he did not know himself. He then went to a staircase which never in his life had he used before—the service staircase, by which his man came to call him every morning; by which, also, presumably, the maids came up later to make his bed and "do the room." These stairs led down to the

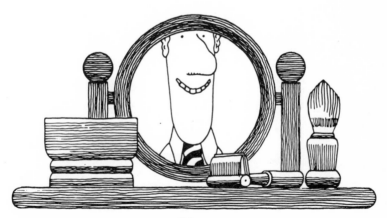

servants' quarters—the kitchens, the pantries, the larders, the wine cellars. He had never been there before, but there must, he supposed, be some way out in that direction if he could only find it.

Presently, as he wandered along a dark passage, he met a footman, one that he faintly recognized as a waiter at the royal table. Adopting an intonation that was not his own, the King said: "Where is that back door that wants seeing to?"

The man stopped in doubt. "I don't know," said he. "Which back door?"

"Oh, any," replied the King. "While I'm here I had better have a look at all of them."

This so disarmed the man's suspicions that he pointed the way to the nearest one. It was not locked. The King opened it and stepped outside. He passed a butcher's boy carrying a basket; the sight of him meant freedom. In another moment he was out in the street. It was a quarter to ten. He asked his way to the police station.

Arriving there, he found an enormous crowd outside clamoring for admittance. Unable to make his way through, he ap-

pealed to a policeman. "I am a witness for the defense," he said.

"What case?" inquired the policeman.

"Oh, 'the Crown case,' I suppose it's called."

Apparently it was. The policeman made way for him. He got in just in time to see his burglar mount to the dock.

When the prosecution had finished, the King went forward and asked to be heard as a witness for the defense.

"What have you got to say?" inquired the magistrate, who, of course, did not recognize him.

"Only to explain that it was I who gave the prisoner those things which he is charged with stealing. I also gave him a hundred pounds for doing it."

This startling statement got him into the witness box. "What is your name?" inquired the Clerk of the Court. "I am the King," said His Majesty. "Lord Almighty!" cried the prisoner, "he's cut off his beard."

The magistrate took one look. A stare of horrified amazement showed recognition of the unbelievable fact that it really was the King. Wonderfully he rose to the occasion.

"Clear the court!" he said. "Remove the prisoner!"

The King was conveyed safely back to the palace in a closed carriage, with a mounted escort. They had their work cut out. Rumor had flown that the King had gone off his head and had shaved it (for this is the way that rumor exaggerates facts), and the crowds that had gathered as a consequence were dense and continuous. It was said that the King had been caught escaping from the country with the crown jewels. Crowds, when they are large enough, will say anything.

This crowd remained gathered outside the palace, a million strong, waiting and hoping for the mad King to show himself.

The King, not really mad—but very much annoyed at not being allowed to give his evidence—was being urgently interviewed by his ministers.

The King said: "If I am not allowed to give evidence I shall abdicate."

"That, Your Majesty," said the Prime Minister, "cannot be allowed. It is unconstitutional."

"It may be unconstitutional," replied the

49

King, "but it is common sense that, if you rob me of my honor, I am no longer a fit person to wear the crown."

The Prime Minister became persuasive. "I only ask Your Majesty, before deciding to do anything, to see a doctor."

"So that he may certify me of unsound mind, I suppose?" replied the King.

The Prime Minister started and looked

confused; but all he said was: "I think if Your Majesty took a little rest—"

"Yes," said the King, "but I warn you, gentlemen, that if you lock me up in my room I shall jump out of the window. I was locked up in my own house today. And it is not to happen again."

And so saying, he went up to his room, and, to make sure, himself locked the door on the inside, leaving the key in the lock.

He looked out of the window. There he saw, stretching away and away before him, enormous crowds, bigger than the crowds on his Coronation Day.

"Well," he thought to himself, "if I do abdicate I shall have plenty of witnesses. And what a funny way of abdicating jumping out of the window will be!"

Then he heard from the drawer where he kept his collars a quick tapping sound which he recognized. It was the Fairy Cotton-Wooleena trying to have her say in the matter.

He went to the drawer and took out the orb. The tapping was still going on.

He gave a tap back from the outside. "Well," he inquired, "what do you want?"

"Let me out!" cried the Fairy angrily. "Let me out, or it shall be the worse for you!"

"If you could have made it the worse for me," replied the King, "you would have done so already."

"Well, haven't I?" cried the Fairy. "Look what a mess you've got into. That's my doing."

"Is it, indeed!" exclaimed the King; the idea had not occurred to him before. "Well, then, if you want to know, on the whole I am enjoying it."

"If you don't take care," said the Fairy, "there will be revolution. And where will you be then?"

"There is going to be revolution," replied the King, "and I am going to make it. I am going to abdicate. And as a first step I am going to get rid of you. There's a big crowd waiting for you. With them you can do what you like; if they want you, they can have you; but I've done with you. You've got to let me alone!"

So saying, he put on his crown for identification, went to the window, and opened it. The crowd greeted his appearance—his very extraordinary appearance—with a hullabaloo of excitement mingled with cheers. Everybody was trying to decide whether he looked as mad as he was reported to be.

The King lifted the hand containing the orb. "Get out of it, if you can!" he said to the Fairy. "But, anyway, get out of this!"

And so saying he hurled the orb as far as

he could into the gaping and expectant crowd.

The Fairy Cotton-Wooleena was three hundred years old and had come to the very end of her days without knowing it. But in her last moments she still had power as of old to work her will, given the opportunity.

Flung out like a bomb—like a bomb the orb burst as it fell, and all the pent-up energies of the Fairy Cotton-Wooleena broke forth: very characteristically they broke forth on an astonished world.

Her productivity in that moment of her dissolution was amazing; how out of one small receptacle she managed it—and that after having had so much of her tail so recently cut off—only a fairy could explain. The Fairy Cotton-Wooleena did it without any explanation whatever—and died of it.

As the orb touched ground and split into small fragments, out of it, like a great puff of smoke, exuded with endless writhings and rollings a billowing volume of cotton-wool. It rose, covering the heads of the crowd; it extended from side to side across the open space before the palace as far as the eye could reach; it drifted in soft piles against the palace wall. And under its effacing touch the crowd became quiet and sleepy, all excitement went out of it, it became as though non-existent, wrapped in cotton-wool, dull, gentle, uninterested; a little encumbered about the legs, it waded back to its homes and its avocations, accepting all that had happened as though it were the right and ordinary thing that everyone would have expected to happen.

It had all been done in a moment—not poison gas or suffocation had caused it: only the spirit of the dying Fairy, temporarily infecting the crowd with a spirit like her own, had caused it, like herself to disperse, pass out, and melt away.

As for the King, when he went back to the door to open it, he found that he had been locked in. That settled the matter. He returned to the window, took off his crown, and, jumping down on to the soft pile of cotton-wool there so conveniently spread to receive him, clambered his way through, and, walking at a quiet pace which attracted nobody's attention reached the street, got upon a bus, and became from that moment an indistinguishable, or at any rate quite unnoticeable, private character like all the rest of us. And a short time after, having found his faithful housekeeper mourning his memory in a little home of her own, he married her. And when I last heard of them they were married still, and were both very happy.

And what about the burglar, you ask, without the King's evidence to defend him? Oh, the burglar was all right; the case was dismissed; in order to hush up the scandal they discharged him. And though Cotton-Wooleena was dead, in official circles her spirit survives and is immortal.

LAURENCE HOUSMAN, the distinguished and often controversial English writer, was born in 1865 in Bromsgrove, Worcestershire. As a young man, he moved to London, where he eventually became art critic on the *Manchester Guardian*. At the same time, he began a career as a poet, playwright, novelist, and essayist. His works, such as *Green Arras, Pains and Penalties, The Chinese Lantern, The Little Plays of St. Francis,* and *Angels and Ministers,* represent much that was best in the literature of his generation. Like his celebrated poet brother, A. E. Housman, who is known today as "the father of modern English poetry," Laurence Housman has enriched the literature of England, America, and the world with his innumerable volumes of plays, poetry, novels, and fantasies. Housman, who never married, died in 1959.